The Body of an American

Dan O'Brien

Inspired in part by the book
Where War Lives by Paul Watson

D1166913

A SAMUEL FRENCH ACTING EDITION

SAMUEL FRENCH

FOUNDED 1830

SAMUELFRENCH.COM
SAMUELFRENCH-LONDON.CO.UK

FOR PRODUCTION ENQUIRIES

UNITED STATES AND CANADA
Info@SamuelFrench.com
1-866-598-8449

UNITED KINGDOM AND EUROPE
Theatre@SamuelFrench-London.co.uk
020-7255-4302

Each title is subject to availability from Samuel French, depending upon country of performance. Please be aware that *THE BODY OF AN AMERICAN* may not be licensed by Samuel French in your territory. Professional and amateur producers should contact the nearest Samuel French office or licensing partner to verify availability.

MUSIC USE NOTE

Licensees are solely responsible for obtaining formal written permission from copyright owners to use copyrighted music in the performance of this play and are strongly cautioned to do so. If no such permission is obtained by the licensee, then the licensee must use only original music that the licensee owns and controls. Licensees are solely responsible and liable for all music clearances and shall indemnify the copyright owners of the play(s) and their licensing agent, Samuel French, against any costs, expenses, losses and liabilities arising from the use of music by licensees. Please contact the appropriate music licensing authority in your territory for the rights to any incidental music.

IMPORTANT BILLING AND CREDIT REQUIREMENTS

If you have obtained performance rights to this title, please refer to your licensing agreement for important billing and credit requirements.

THE BODY OF AN AMERICAN was first produced at Portland Center Stage in Portland, Oregon on October 2, 2012. The performance was directed by Bill Rauch, with sets and costumes by Christopher Acebo, lighting by James F. Ingalls, projections by Eamonn Farrell, and sound by Casi Pacilio and Eamonn Farrell. The Production Stage Manager was Jeremy Eisen. The cast was as follows:

PAUL . . . . William Salyers
DAN . . . . Danny Wolohan

The Body of an American is winner of the inaugural Edward M. Kennedy Prize for Drama, the Horton Foote Prize, the PEN Center USA Award for Drama, and the L. Arnold Weissberger Award

The play was commissioned and developed with support from The Playwrights' Center's 2009-2010 McKnight Commission and Residency Program, Minneapolis, MN

Additional support was received from the Rockefeller Foundation Bellagio Residency, a Future Collaborations Grant from Theatre Communications Group, a Sundance Institute Time Warner Storytelling Fellowship, the 2010 PlayLabs at The Playwrights' Center, the 2011 New Harmony Project, a workshop at Pioneer Theatre in 2011, and the 2011 JAW Festival at Portland Center Stage

CHARACTERS

Two actors play all the roles here – ideally one actor in his 30s, who plays
DAN most of the time, and an actor in his 50s to mostly play **PAUL**.

The older of these two actors has the first line of the play, and with each
new character-heading the actors alternate.

PLACE & TIME

Scenes 1-7: various.

Scenes 8-10: the Arctic, the present.

AUTHOR'S NOTES

The stage directions within the script are suggestions of photographs,
maps, moving images, etc., to be projected somewhere prominent
onstage; as well as suggestions for occasional sound design. All of the
photographs listed are by Paul Watson or the playwright or unknown,
except where noted.

All of the photographs listed are by Paul Watson or the playwright or
unknown, except where noted, and can be obtained by contacting
the author's agent: Beth Blickers, Abrams Artists Agency, 275 Seventh
Avenue, 26th Floor, New York, NY 10001.

I do want to hear this because
you're another person in this story.
Um, and each, each person in this story
ends up telling his own story of what
I call – the working title for the book
I'm writing is *Where War Lives*. From a quote
of Albert Camus when he was keeping
his notebooks pre-World War Two. And a friend
wrote to him saying, you know, I'm grappling
with this philosophical question, Where
does this vile thing, war, live? And Camus said,
he's in Algiers at the time and he says,

I look at the bright blue sky and I think
of the guilt that I feel from not being
in a position where I, I can die
with them, while at the same time wanting to
be as far away as I can from it.

—Paul Watson in conversation with Dr. Joseph LeDoux, January 2006

1: Fresh Air

PAUL.   My name's Paul Watson.

PAUL.   I'm Paul Watson.

TERRY GROSS.   This
is Fresh Air,

TERRY GROSS.   I'm Terry Gross. Remember
that famous 1993 photo?

PAUL.   I was a reporter who happened to—

DAN.   Dear Mr. Watson. I don't usually
email strangers like this.

TERRY GROSS.   This is Fresh Air.

DAN.   I was leaving Princeton.

PAUL.   New Jersey?

DAN.   Where
I had this fellowship.

PAUL.   You had a what?

DAN.   A residency—

PAUL.   Which means you do what?

DAN.   Well
I was supposed to write a play.

PAUL.   A play.

DAN.   Yes.

PAUL.   About what?

DAN.   Ghosts.

PAUL.   Ghosts?

DAN.   Yeah. Ghosts.

PAUL.   What kind
of ghosts?

DAN.   Historical, ghosts.

PAUL.   And they pay you
          for this?

DAN.   Sort of. Definitely. I'm really
          grateful to them—

PAUL.   Is it scary?

DAN.   My play?
          I don't know. I hope so. To me it was.

TERRY GROSS. This is Fresh Air,

TERRY GROSS.   I'm Terry Gross. Let's start
          with a description of that now famous
          Pulitzer prize-winning photo:

PAUL.   I was
          a reporter who happened to carry
          a camera, a 35 mm
          Nikon I bought because my editors
          wouldn't buy me one.

PAUL.   We were on the roof
          of the Sahafi, where the journalists
          were staying,

PAUL.   *if* they were staying.

PAUL.   You could count
          on one hand who was still there.

PAUL.   I'd have to
          count on one hand because my other hand

PAUL.   isn't really a hand at all.

PAUL.   I was
          born this way.

PAUL.   A bunch of us were drinking
          beer.

PAUL.   Did you see that light?

REPORTER.   What light?

PAUL.   Behind
          that chopper there. It just went down behind
          that hill.

DAN. Chaos ensues. *[Image: white light.]*

PAUL. A 16-hour battle raged through the night between US Army rangers, special ops, Delta Force and Somali militias. It started as an arrest operation trying to abduct commanders in Mohamed Aideed's militia. They were trying to track down Aideed and arrest him for allegedly organizing attacks on UN peacekeepers.

PAUL. When I woke up on the hotel floor, still dressed, hung over,

PAUL. 18 American soldiers had been killed and 75 wounded.

PAUL. Clouds of smoke billowing up from burning tire barricades, dead bodies in the street.

PAUL. American troops were trying to get the rest of their force back alive, and in so doing they'd killed more than 600 Somalis so far,

PAUL. including women and children, huddled in the darkness as bullets or shrapnel pierced the tin walls of their shacks.

PAUL. Gutale's my translator. He hurries through the gate:

GUTALE. They are shooting everything that moves now, even donkeys!

PAUL. He gets 30 dollars a day.

PAUL. My driver and bodyguard get a hundred.

PAUL.   That's always been the hardest
                        part of my job: convincing good people
                        who get none of a byline's ego boost
                        to risk their lives because I've decided
                        a story's worth dying for.

GUTALE.   They're shooting
                        people on sight! Even people with no
                        weapons!

PAUL.   Mogadishu was beautiful
                        once, white-painted Italianate villas
                        in the capitol of the most stable
                        state in Africa.

PAUL.   Now you see women
                        grocery shopping with militias firing
                        machine guns up and down the avenue,

PAUL.   children playing on the front lines, running
                        water and bullets beside their mothers
                        to keep the gunmen supplied.

GUTALE.   They shot down
                        a Black Hawk! They are taking a soldier
                        with them from street to street, perhaps alive,
                        perhaps dead!

PAUL.   They threw me in the back seat
                        of the car,

PAUL.   a Toyota Cressida
                        that nobody outside of the safe zone
                        would recognize,

PAUL.   and made me hide my face
                        between Gutale and my body guard
                        Mohamed.

PAUL.   With another Mohamed
                        driving, and a gunman in front cradling
                        an AK-47,

PAUL.   we drove through
                the gates and crawled from street to street. Passing
                the corpse-collectors, men carrying bodies
                by their hands and feet, glaring at us through
                the filthy windshield.

GUTALE.   Has anyone seen
                a captured American soldier?

PAUL.   Some said,

GUTALE.   They've seen him. He says he's alive, tied up
                in a wheelbarrow.

PAUL.   A wheelbarrow?

GUTALE.   No,
                this man says he's dead. He's most definitely
                dead.

PAUL.   I took a few pictures of some kids
                bouncing up and down on a rotor blade
                in the smoldering tail section of that downed
                Black Hawk.

GUTALE.   Have you seen the American
                soldier?

PAUL.   The entire crowd pointed,

GUTALE.   This way.

PAUL.   Each time a Black Hawk thundered past people
                would shake their fists and curse at it.

PAUL.   We drove
                all over the city for two hours and
                were about to give up,

PAUL.   when the driver
                makes a u-turn.

GUTALE.   He sees something.

PAUL.   A mob
                of 200 Somalis, moving down
                an alleyway.

GUTALE.   What is it?

MOHAMED.   This is bad,
too dangerous.

GUTALE.   Go slowly.

PAUL.   What's he saying?

GUTALE.   He's a coward. He's worried about his
car.

MOHAMED.   This guy's going to get us killed!

GUTALE.   Shut up!

PAUL.   Gutale gets out:

GUTALE.   Gamay's in the car,
you know Gamay!

PAUL.   Gamay is local slang
for cripple.

GUTALE.   Little man! No hand! He's not
American, he's Canadian! You know
Gamay. He just wants to take some pictures.
Can he?

PAUL.   The crowd parts around me.

PAUL.   I look
down at the street:

PAUL.   and I meet Staff Sgt.
William David Cleveland.

GUTALE.   Take the picture
quickly.

PAUL.   I've taken pictures of corpses
before, many of them much more fucked up
than this man.

GUTALE.   Hurry, Paul!

PAUL.   I bend over,
shoulders stiff.

GUTALE.   Take it now!

PAUL.   With a camera
        in front of your eye, you cover your face
        and you focus only on the good shot.

PAUL.   You shut everything else out.

PAUL.   Everything
        goes quiet.

PAUL.   Despite the noise of the crowd
        and the helicopters,

PAUL.   everything goes
        completely silent. And I hear a voice
        both in my head and out:

CLEVELAND.   If you do this,
        I will own you forever.

PAUL.   I'm sorry
        but I have to.

CLEVELAND.   If you do this, I will
        own you.

PAUL.   I've sought psychiatric treatment
        in subsequent years. And my psychiatrist
        says it's my superego. I believe
        it was William David Cleveland speaking
        to me.

TERRY GROSS.   And what did he mean?

PAUL.   Well, Terry,
        I took it as a warning.

TERRY GROSS.   A warning
        of what exactly?

PAUL.   I have to do this.

PAUL.   I don't want to do this.

PAUL.   I don't want to
        desecrate your body.

CLEVELAND.   If you do this
        I will own you forever.

PAUL.   I took his
picture.

PAUL.   While they were beating his body
and cheering. Some spitting.

PAUL.   Some kid wearing
a chopper crewman's goggles shoves his way
into the frame. His face is all screwed up
in rapturous glee while giving the dead man
the finger.

[Image: Paul Watson's full-length photograph of Staff Sgt. William David Cleveland.]

PAUL.   An old man's raising his cane
like a club and thudding it down against
the dead flesh.

PAUL.   Wind's blowing dirt and the stench
is making me gag.

PAUL.   For weeks I'd hated
UN peacekeepers like this man, who killed
from the sky with impunity.

PAUL.   But now
it was us against them.

GUTALE.   Get in the car,
Gamay!

PAUL.   The men holding the ropes that bind
the soldier's wrists are stretching his arms out
over his head.

PAUL.   They're rolling his body
back and forth in the hammering morning light.

PAUL.   I feel like I'm standing beside myself.

PAUL.   I feel like I'm somebody else watching
myself take these photographs,

PAUL.   somebody
named Paul, doing this crazy thing,

PAUL.   shooting
pictures.

PAUL.   Asking, Did I put the batteries
in?

PAUL.   *Click.*   *[Image: another*

PAUL.   The bullet wounds are in his legs: *shot from*
                did they shoot him in the street, did he die   *this series.]*
                before he crashed?

PAUL.   *Click.*   *[Image: another*

PAUL.   His body's so limp   *shot.]*
                he must have just died.

PAUL.   *Click.*   *[Image: another*

PAUL.   Maybe he's still   *shot.]*
                alive? Is that why I can hear his voice?
                If you do this,

PAUL.   *Click. Click.*   *[Image: another*

PAUL.   I will own you.   *shot.]*

PAUL.   *Click. Click. Click. Click.*

PAUL.   *[Image: another*
                                    You poor man. Who are you? *shot.]*

GUTALE.   We must go. Let's go. They don't want us here
                anymore.

PAUL.   The car door's shut.

PAUL.   Soft idling
                of the engine. The muffled mob.

PAUL.   It's like
                I've stepped out of Mogadishu into

PAUL.   a wobbling canoe years ago in   *[Moving image:*
                Sudan,   *water at dusk.]*

PAUL.   drifting downriver at dusk with

ANDREW.   Andrew Stawicki,

PAUL.   a Polish émigré
                photographer who snaps a picture of
                boys running naked like a snake along
                the river's blood-red spine. That's going to be
                a great picture.

ANDREW.   They won't print it.

PAUL.   Why not?

ANDREW.   The kid's dick is showing!

PAUL.   In my mind's eye
I see Sgt. Cleveland's Army-issue
green underwear, the only clothing left
on his body.

PAUL.   The underwear's slightly   [Image: Paul's
askew, so you can just make out a piece   full-body shot.]
of the dead man's scrotum.

PAUL.   Open the door!
Open it!

PAUL.   This time I framed it better:
the body from the waist up.

PAUL.   A woman   [Image: Paul's
slapping him with a flattened can.   famous half-
                                                    body shot.]

PAUL.   That boy
with the goggles shoveling his face through
the mob,

PAUL.   laughing at us.

PAUL.   Men with bloodshot
eyes notice me.

PAUL.   It would be like squashing
a cockroach to kill me, this infidel
who can't take a hint.

GUTALE.   Look, he's leaving now!
See? We're leaving for good! Thank you!

PAUL.   The squeak
of the hotel gate always let me breathe
easier. As if a few sleepy guards could
actually keep us safe from everything
happening out there.

PAUL.   I take the service stairs
two at a time to my room, stuff the roll
of film between the mattress and box spring,
switch on the broken AC,

PAUL. and collapse
on my bed with my eyes closed and I cry
for a very long time.

TERRY GROSS. This is *Fresh Air*.
The AP printed it, and so did *Time*
magazine.

PAUL. That's right. AP moved the half
-body shots, which appeared in newspapers
all over the world. What *Time* magazine
did, which I find fascinating, is they
digitally altered the underwear
so you can't see any genitals. But
you do see horrific desecration
of an American soldier.

TERRY GROSS. This picture
had incredible impact.

PAUL. Yes, Terry,
that's right. Because immediately the heat
was on President Bill Clinton to do
something. And that something was to announce
the immediate withdrawal of American
troops. Then, when it became time to decide
whether or not the United States should
lead an intervention in Rwanda,
where 800,000 people were killed
in a hundred days, President Clinton
decided not to use the word genocide
so we wouldn't be *forced* to intervene.
And we know without a doubt Al-Qaeda
was there in Mogadishu. It says so
on indictments in US Federal Court,
bin Laden's bragged about it, his minions
have bragged about it. But what disturbs me

the most is that Al-Qaeda learned a lot
from the propaganda impact of that
photograph. 18 American soldiers
were killed that day. Which is nothing compared
to what used to happen on a bad day
in Vietnam. And it's only relatively
bad compared to what's still happening these days
in Iraq, or Afghanistan. I think
it's safe to say, take all of the events
that happened, but remove the photograph,
and Al-Qaeda would not have chased us out
of Somalia, bin Laden would not have
been able to say to his followers, Look
we're able to do this, we only need
small victories to defeat history's greatest
military. After my photograph:
9/11, and this never-ending
war on terror.

TERRY GROSS.   My guest today has been
war reporter Paul Watson. His memoir
about reporting from war zones is called
Where War Lives.

TERRY GROSS.   We'll talk more after a break.

2: Who Was He Talking To?

DAN.   I was listening to this podcast. Writing   *[Google map:*
my play about historical ghosts. Packing   *Princeton, NJ.]*
up all our things. It was the very end
of August. It was the end of New York
for us. It was the end of something else,
what? our youth? In Princeton. Which is just so
beautiful this time of year. Every time
of year, really. All the trees and leaves. All

the squirrels. All of the privileged children,
including myself, in some ways. I was
sad to leave. It had been a rough few years.
I'd walk around the campus late at night
and feel almost good about myself. Smart.
Of value. And of course I felt guilty
too, to have had this library. These trees
and squirrels. The beautiful young women
to watch. Unlimited laser printing.
While you're off in Iraq, Paul. Or Kabul.
Or Jakarta, that's where you live, Paul, right?   *[Google*
And Jakarta's in Indonesia. Right?   *map: Jakarta.]*
There was this hangar-sized Whole Foods nearby,   *[Video*
lots of Priuses, and bumper stickers   *image:*
celebrating the date when Bush would leave   *verdant*
office. I'd go running in thunderstorms   *window in*
sometimes. I'd sit on the back porch sipping   *Princeton.]*
vodka, cooking meat on a charcoal grill.
Watching swallows swoop out of a twilit
sky into my maple tree. And your voice
got to me. It's your voice:

PAUL.   I tend to be
solitary.

DAN.   This is you speaking, though
it might as well be me.

PAUL.   I like to stay
home with my wife and son.

DAN.   Dinner parties?

PAUL.   I tend to stay away. I've spent enough
time around people who do what I do,
and in my opinion, and I include
myself foremost in this group, we're a bunch
of misfits, people who are seeking self
-esteem through risk.

DAN.   I felt you could have been
talking about playwrights. Without any
real risk. You were mad:

PAUL.   I'm sick of being
lied to. And I take it as a challenge
to make sure nobody's lying to me.

DAN. I felt like I knew you. Or I was you
in some alternate reality.

PAUL.   Men
start wars because it helps them to make sure
that women aren't laughing at them.

DAN.   You
were funny. Sort of.

PAUL.   I'm more comfortable
with the weak than I am the powerful,
growing up in this condition.

DAN.   We should
talk about that, your hand.

PAUL.   Should we?

DAN.   Why not?

PAUL. It's helped me out a lot. In Kosovo
in food lines, they'd think I was a wounded
war vet and give me all kinds of free stuff.

DAN. And as I'm packing and listening to you
I'm wondering if I feel so moved because
you sound so messed up,

PAUL.   If something's risky
and we probably shouldn't do it, I'll say,
Don't worry about me, I'm already
dead.

DAN.   Or because you scare me. The haunted
often sound like ghosts, in my experience.

PAUL. I just have this sense I've already lived
much longer than I should have.

[Image: Paul Watson preparing to take a photo; his deformed hand is prominent. (Andrew Stawicki)]

DAN.
                                      You poor man,
who are you?

3: Q&A. Or, Got To Go

PAUL. I have no idea who my father was. *[Image: Watson*
DAN. He was a soldier, right? *Family photo,*
PAUL.   I've got to go. *1960; Paul is*
Take care. Paul. *in the baby*
DAN.   I just wanted to say thanks *stroller.]*
for writing me back. I got your email
on my wife's BlackBerry halfway across
the country, at this tumbleweed rest stop
on an Indian reservation somewhere
outside Tulsa.

PAUL.   Dear Dan, I just got back
from Kabul. Where I found out it's easy *[Google map:*
to buy stolen US military *Kabul.]*
flash drives at an Afghan bazaar outside *[Images: ID*
Bagram air base. And these flash drives are full *photos of*
of classified information, social *US soldiers,*
security numbers of soldiers, maps *maps of air*
of Taliban and Al-Qaeda targets *strikes in*
in both Afghanistan and Pakistan. *Afghanistan*
DAN. Wow. *and Pakistan,*
PAUL.   Sorry, what were we talking about? *2008.]*
DAN. Your dad.
PAUL.   Stormed the beach at Normandy. Died
a few days shy of my second birthday.
DAN. And you were born when?
PAUL.   1959.
How old are you, Dan?

DAN.   I'm younger than you.
I could be your nephew, or a younger
brother maybe.

PAUL.   My father didn't die
in the war though.

DAN.   Of course not. How did he?

PAUL.   He had PKD, or Polycystic
Kidney Disease.

DAN.   Which is what?

PAUL.   Like it sounds:
cysts start growing all over your kidneys
till eventually you die. I have it
too.

DAN.   Will it kill you?

PAUL.   I've got pills for it.

DAN.   So, what you mean when you say you don't know
who your dad was, is you don't remember
him?

PAUL.   Do you?

DAN.   Do I remember my dad?

PAUL.   Do you know who he is?

DAN.   What do you mean?

PAUL.   What did you think I meant?

DAN.   He was around.
I mean my father was always around,
every day. He never spoke to us. If
he did, well then it was just to tell you
how fucking stupid you were.

PAUL.   Is he dead?

DAN.   I don't know.

PAUL.   You don't know?

DAN.   Wait why are you
asking *me* questions?

PAUL.   I've got to get back
to Kabul. I'll email you.

DAN.   I'm staying
in this condo in a renovated
schoolhouse. Sometimes I hear ghostly children
laughing. This gland in my neck is swollen
and aches. I'm Googling the symptoms. Let's Skype
or Facebook. Are you on Facebook?

PAUL.   I don't
know why but I'd rather keep emailing
like this. I don't know why. But it's almost
like a conversation.

DAN.   Yeah but it's not
a conversation.

PAUL.   Yeah but it's almost.
Are you in LA?

DAN.   I'm in Madison,   *[Google map:*
Wisconsin.   *Madison, WI.]*

PAUL.   What? Why?

DAN.   Teaching.

PAUL.   And writing
about ghosts?

DAN.   Sure. Still.

PAUL.   Is it snowing there?   *[Moving*

DAN.   It hasn't stopped snowing since I touched down   *image:*
in January. Cars are abandoned   *falling*
in the middle of highways. I don't leave   *snow.]*
the condo much.

PAUL.   I'm home in Jakarta,   *[Moving*
in case you're wondering. There's a thunderstorm   *image:*
and my little boy's asleep. He's always   *lightning,*
asking me, How long will you be gone. Dad?   *rain.]*
He's seven, so he doesn't understand

time just yet. Few weeks back we were lying
in bed together and he asked me, When
you're dead will you still be watching me? Where
were we?

DAN.   We were talking about fathers.

PAUL.   So then Ray enlisted at 17,

DAN.   You call him Ray?

PAUL.   faked his eye test. He was,

SOMEONE.   Tall. Splendid physique.   *[Image: family*

PAUL.   That's what someone wrote   *photo*
about him, in one of his files. It said,   *again, Paul's*
Ray is: *tall father.]*

SOMEONE.   Frank. Pleasant manner. Decisive
style of thinking.

PAUL.   This one story I know,
there's only one story I know for sure,
they were taking a medieval city
in France, twisted streets, churches and houses   *[Map:*
made of stone. My father takes a bullet   *Villons-les-buissons,*
in his thigh. Watches one of his soldiers   *France, 1944.]*
trapped in the long grass. Ray can't do a thing
but watch his friend die. Each time this man cries
out for help, a Nazi sniper shoots him
till he's dead.

DAN.   How do you know this?

PAUL.   Research.
My mother told me.

DAN.   Yes. Good. What's she like?

PAUL.   She's the strongest woman I know.

DAN.   Okay,
fine. What else?

PAUL.   They were sitting together
on a streetcar. The bang of a pothole
and he's gone. She gets off at the next stop

and walks home, and sits down on the front step.
And waits for him.

DAN.   Sounds like PTSD.

PAUL.   I've got to cut this one short.

DAN.   Can we talk
about your hand again?

PAUL.   My hand?

DAN.   You know,
your lack of a hand.

PAUL.   I'll be in Sulu,
in the Philippines.

DAN.   Outside my window   *[Moving image:*
a freight train rolls past every night. Its bell   *snow falling.]*
tolls over and over again.

PAUL.   Seven
civilians have been killed by Philippine
troops, including two children.

DAN.   as the snow
piles higher on Lake Monona, burying
the sign Obama stuck in the ice: *Yes
We Can!*

PAUL.   Reading glasses, check. Sensible
shoes, check.

DAN.   Spring break.   *[Image: bright light.]*

PAUL.   —Hey, Dan! You were asking
about my hand. It doesn't bother me
much. My mother used to always tell me,
Nobody's perfect!

DAN.   How'd it get that way?

PAUL.   The kids would crowd around me at recess
and the bravest ones would reach out and touch
my stump,

KID.   How'd it get that way, Paul? Huh? Huh?

PAUL.   This was when I remember first thinking:
This is not me.

PAUL.   This, that body belongs
to somebody else.

PAUL.   The day I was born
I had these nubbins instead of fingers   *[Image: that*

PAUL.   and the doctor just snipped them off.   *picture*

PAUL.   The hand's   *again of*
                                                        Paul
attached to a wrist that bends, with a palm   *preparing to take*
no bigger than an infant's.   *a photograph.*

DAN.   Did your mom   *(Stawicki)]*
take thalidomide?

PAUL.   ·   Everyone thinks that,
but no she didn't. It's a mystery,
something in the DNA.

DAN.   Is that why
you're like this?

PAUL.   Like what, Dan?

DAN.   Oh I don't know,
a war reporter?

PAUL.   iPod, check. Satellite
phone, check. Laptop, check. Endless tangles of
cable, check.

DAN.   Two people have been murdered
near where I'm staying,

PAUL.   Some bars of Dettol,   *[Image: Joel*
disinfectant soap for microbes.   *Anthony*
                                                        Marino.]
DAN.   a man
my age. A girl. On different days.

PAUL.   Check.

DAN.   Both   *[Image:*
were stabbed repeatedly. In the middle   *Brittany*
of the day, at home. I go out running   *Zimmermann.]*
on the icy roads past their stained faces

on telephone poles. Just like I used to
jog past the makeshift morgue outside Bellevue
that long-ago September.

PAUL.   Sorry, Dan,
I've been out of touch. I was in Christchurch
on vacation. Where were we?

DAN.   Your perfect
childhood.

PAUL.   Yes, my street was Princess Margaret
Boulevard, my school was Princess Margaret   *[Google map:*
Public School.   *Princess*

DAN.   Who's Princess Margaret again?   *Margaret*

PAUL. We had a milkman, mailman, paperboy.   *Blvd.,*

DAN. How many siblings did you have?   *Etobicoke,*

PAUL.   Four. You?   *Ontario,*

DAN. Five.   *Canada.]*

PAUL.   Wow, you really are Irish!

DAN.   Nothing
bad happened in your childhood? other than
your absent father and your absent hand
that never bothered you?

PAUL.   My brother Jim
liked to take my father's old Lugar out
of hiding. Sometimes he'd let me hold it
and I'd imagine myself as the man
who'd once held his finger on that trigger.

DAN. You mean your father?

PAUL.   No, the dead Nazi
he got it from!

DAN.   Did you have any friends?
You sound lonely. You sound kind of like this
really lonely kid.

PAUL.   I was in a band
called Eruption? I was the manager
of the band, because of my hand. We did
a shitload of drugs: Purple Microdot,   [Music: Pink
California Sunshine—   Floyd's "Brain

DAN.   What's that, acid?   Damage."]

PAUL.   My best friend Richard and I listening
to *Dark Side of the Moon* in the middle   [Image: Paul
of this circle we'd burnt into a field   Watson as a
of grass behind my house, high as two kites.   teenager in the
Richard turned me on to Camus. We'd chew   '70s: plaid
peyote before gym class   bow tie, plaid
                                                         pants.
PAUL.   and get off   Long hair.]
on the psychedelic rainbows trailing
behind high-jumpers and kids doing flips
off balance beams.

PAUL.   Oh, I remember one
thing that was somewhat disturbing: our friend
Andy blew his brains out at his parents'
summer cottage.

DAN.   Just somewhat disturbing?

PAUL.   It was hardly surprising. He was stuck
outside himself.

DAN.   Were you, Paul?

PAUL.   I hung out
with this dealer, he must've been 30.
At a motel he pulls out a bottle
and a baggie full of pills. Up or down,
my choice. I wash down a few with a belt
of whiskey.

DRUG DEALER.   You took some heavy downers,
man.

PAUL.   Who cares?

DRUG DEALER.   That's the trouble with chicks, right?

PAUL.   Right!

DRUG DEALER.   Hells yeah!

PAUL.   An hour later he's carving
his arm with his knife.

DRUG DEALER.   Bitches always want
perfection!

PAUL.   Then he's slinging my body
over his back like I'm some medevaced
soldier on TV in Vietnam. Dumping
me in a taxi.

DRUG DEALER.   He's my little bro,
man. Just take him home.

PAUL.   Alone and puking
through the chain link of a construction site
as the taxi spits gravel.

DAN.   You were fucked   [Image:
up, Paul. Maybe you were depressed. Maybe   close-up of
you were low on some brain chemical like   that photo
serotonin, dopamine, whatever,   of Paul as
and this kind of crazy behavior was   a teenager in
your way of feeling normal.   the '70s.]

PAUL.   But I was
also having fun. Didn't you have fun
in high school, Dan?

DAN.   Sorry, I've got to go
teach. My students are trying to learn how
to write with conflict and stakes and something
remotely real.

PAUL.   I had this one teacher
I loved. He took us all on a field trip
once. There we were floating in our canoes   [Moving
in Algonquin Provincial Park, under   image: river
a canopy of stars. With my classmate   at night.
Stephen Harper, future Prime Minister,   Stars.]

no kidding, paddling behind. Thinking, Who
could *not* love Albert Camus? And that's how
I ended up winning the Pulitzer.

DAN. Wait. What? I don't get it—

PAUL.   I've got to go,
this time it's an emergency. Turn on   *[Google map:*
your TV and you'll see.   *Burma.]*

DAN.   I've got to say,
Paul, I can't help feeling you're not being
entirely honest with me here. I mean,
I don't mean that you're lying, per se. But
everything has this kind of Hemingway
patina to it. This kind of old school
journalistic swagger. It's like you're trying
to impress me.

PAUL.   I got into Burma
on a tourist visa. With the Tribune
execs measuring the column inches
we produce, not getting into Burma
to cover the cyclone devastation
would've been career suicide. Hiding
by day in the hull of a riverboat
in the Irrawaddy Delta. Among
the hundreds of corpses bobbing at dusk
in the sea-soaked paddies is the body
of a child. In pajama bottoms with   *[Image: this*
teddy bear cartoons on them. The bleached skin's   *image,*
like rotting rattan. The leg bones are green.   *perhaps.]*
The stench is unbearable, but the people
on shore don't seem to notice. My fixer
explains that Buddhists believe the body   *[Moving image:*
FIXER. is nothing more than an empty vessel,   *river at night.*
and the soul has already been reborn   *Stars.]*
as someone new.

PAUL.   After several stiff drinks
that night I lay on the roof of our boat
staring up at the universe,

PAUL.   listening
to Laura Bush give forth with earnest pleas
to the junta on Voice of America,

PAUL.   and I imagined myself as nothing
more than a passenger on this rotting
vessel of my body. And it felt good,
I felt free.

DAN.   That freight train's approaching fast,
its headlamp swallowing the churning snow.
The chiming bell, the shrieking horn—

PAUL.   Dear Dan,
I've been meaning to say: you sound kind of
depressed. Don't let that get ahold of you.
Trust me. Maybe you should talk to someone
besides me? Or take a pill. Has it stopped
snowing yet?   *[Moving image:*

DAN.   Nope.   *falling snow.]*

PAUL.   Medication. Calculate
estimated time away, multiply
by seven pills a day for depression,
blood pressure, PKD. Toss in extra
in case I get kidnapped. Check.

DAN.   Where are you
going this time, Paul?

PAUL.   A few chocolate bars:
85 percent cocoa, for the dose
of flavonoids the TV doctor says
will give me an extra 3.5 years
and fight heart plaque.

DAN.   Where are you now?

PAUL.   My son
             is sleeping. It's the rainy season here
             again and lightning's lighting up his face
             like a strobe. I lean in close to his ear
             and whisper,

PAUL.   Don't be afraid.

PAUL.   I'll come back
             home soon.

PAUL.   Do not be afraid.

PAUL.   Japanese
             green tea for the antioxidants. Corkscrew
             for the cheap Bordeaux I'll purchase en route
             at Duty Free,

DAN.   I've got some more questions
             for you, Paul—

PAUL.   more antioxidants and
             some liquid courage to help ease the pain
             of these five-star hotel room blues.

4: The Ghosts Are Getting Closer

             But I'm whining, Dan.

DAN.   Okay, let's get back
             to the story. You win the Pulitzer
             Prize.

PAUL.   I was in Rwanda when I heard
             the news. As everybody's aware now,
             300 Tutsis an hour were being
             beaten to death with these large wooden clubs
             with bent nails and heavy spikes sticking out
             of them. Real prehistoric shit. Homemade
             machetes. Just a few thousand UN
             soldiers with air support could've washed all
             those maggots away.

PAUL.   We were getting high   *[Moving image,*
on the bridge over Rusumo Falls.   *sound: waterfall.]*

PAUL.   We
is not the royal we, we is someone
I don't want you to meet just yet.

PAUL.   Khareen
and I watching refugees spill over
the border to Tanzania. Watching
corpses spill over the waterfall down
into this brown whirlpool, smashing against
the rocks.

PAUL.   In a house we found children piled   *[Sound:*
like sandbags on a bed.   *flies buzzing.]*

PAUL.   There's a baby
down at the bottom. Its tiny hand is
bloated, its severed head cracked open like
an eggshell. Did the older children try
to hide him in here?

PAUL.   Outside the back door
I slipped on a bunch of school books. One book
had been covered neatly with a color
publicity shot of the *Dynasty*
show cast. With John Forsythe's fucking
grinning face.

PAUL.   The ghosts are getting closer.

PAUL.   In Gahini, a 16-year-old named
François Sempundu sat on the grimy
brown foam of his hospital bed.

TRANSLATOR.   He says
Hutus hacked up his mother and siblings.
He says he hid beneath the kitchen sink
for a week, beside his family's rotting
corpses.

PAUL.   François Sempundu was speaking
             so calmly.

TRANSLATOR.   He says, By then if someone
             had come to kill me I wouldn't have cared
             much.   *[Sound: cicadas,*
                                                      crickets.]

PAUL.   At a church near Nyarubuye
             we pushed open a gate on a courtyard
             like Auschwitz. Like Sarajevo. They'd come here
             hoping God would protect them somehow, but
             it only made things that much easier
             to get butchered.

PAUL.   In Zaire a girl stands
             at the roadside. Rows of buzzing corpses.

PAUL.   At a Rwandan refugee camp.

PAUL.   She's
             looking for the toilet,

PAUL.   which was a field
             where a hundred thousand people would shit
             and piss and die.

PAUL.   This girl stumbles barefoot
             into a ditch of bodies, some rolled up
             in reed mats. She's looking everywhere and
             now she begins to cry.

PAUL.   As if hoping   *[Sound: this child*
             somebody will help her.   *crying, as*
PAUL.   But nobody's   *if far away.]*
             coming.

PAUL.   I thought to myself, This would make
             a great picture.

PAUL.   This is a beautiful
             picture, somehow.

PAUL. I raised my camera, stepped
backwards to frame her with more corpses and *[Image:*
I stepped on a dead old woman's arm. *this child*

PAUL. It *lost*
snaps like a stick. *among*

corpses of
PAUL. Then a few days later *Rwandan*
I'm at Columbia University's *refugees in*
Low Memorial Library. In this room *Zaire.]*
like the Parthenon and the Pantheon
confused. Cornucopias of hors d'oeuvres
on aproned banquet tables, wearing tight shoes
and a navy blazer, wool slacks picked out
this morning at Brooks Brothers. John Honderich,
my boss at the *Star*—

HONDERICH. Watson, you don't look
so hot.

PAUL. I guess I just feel bad about
that soldier's family.

HONDERICH. Have you thought about
finding his wife, or his mother? hunting
them down?

PAUL. Had I?

PAUL. Had I?

PAUL. Kevin Carter,
who just last month was snorting Ritalin
off the floor of my apartment before
rocketing off into the townships,

PAUL. wins
for feature photography:

PAUL. a vulture
waiting for a Sudanese girl to die.

PAUL. Always a popular category.

PAUL.   Carter comes back to the table:

CARTER.   Hear that
applause, Watson? I kicked your arse!

PAUL.   Two months
later I'm back in Rwanda. Honderich
calls me on my satellite phone:

HONDERICH.   Carter
killed himself last night. Parked his pickup truck
in Johannesburg, duct-taped a garden hose
to the tail pipe. Left a suicide note

PAUL.   that I'll paraphrase:

CARTER.   I have been haunted so
now I'll haunt you.

HONDERICH.   Paul?

HONDERICH.   Paul?

PAUL.   I don't care about
him.

PAUL.   —Who cares?

PAUL.   I don't care!

PAUL.   With so many
people suffering all over the world
who want nothing more than to live—?

PAUL.   That man
is a coward!

PAUL.   If you can't do your job
then get out of the way so someone else
can.

PAUL.   Of course I've wanted to kill myself
before. But the truth is I've always lacked
the courage.

PAUL.   So I tell myself:

PAUL.   Just go
someplace dangerous. Let somebody else
kill you.

5: Shrinking

GRINKER. O-kay. So. You are 35 years old,
you are male. You are a reporter for
the *Toronto Star*, and you're stationed here
in Johannesburg.

PAUL.   You have a real talent   *[Image:*
for stating the obvious.   *dark bookcase.]*

GRINKER.   Are you shaking?

PAUL. Am I?

GRINKER.   You have sweat all over your face!

PAUL. Let me catch my breath.

GRINKER.   O-kay.

PAUL.   It's just that
I've never been to a psychiatrist
before.

GRINKER.   And what are you scared will happen
to you?

PAUL.   I'll lose my edge.

GRINKER.   What does that mean,
your edge?

PAUL.   Being crazy.

GRINKER.   You think I could
cure you of that?

PAUL.   Being somewhat crazy
is a requirement in my line of work.

GRINKER. If you leave I won't charge you anything.
You wouldn't be the first to change his mind
about psychiatry. But you called me, Paul,
and told me you've been feeling paranoid—

PAUL. That's not a psychiatric disorder,
in my opinion. People don't deserve
to be trusted.

GRINKER.   You are irritable,
                small things will make you cry. Interestingly
                you deny nightmares. No psychiatric
                history prior to this. Congenitally
                deformed arm. Don't smoke. Self-medicating
                with lots of alcohol, marijuana—

PAUL.   Look
                all I want from you is some feel-good pills
                to patch me up. "O-kay"?

GRINKER.   O-kay. We can
                find you something, I'm sure.

PAUL.   Thank you.

GRINKER.   But first
                you'll need to talk to me. Medication
                targets symptoms: we will need to target
                your soul as well. You find that funny?

PAUL.   Yes.

GRINKER.   What's your mother like, Paul?

PAUL.   She's the strongest
                woman I know.

GRINKER.   And have you known many
                women?

PAUL.   One.

GRINKER.   You've known only one woman?

PAUL.   I've been in a relationship with one
                woman. On and off. Khareen.

GRINKER.   Careen?

PAUL.   Ha!

GRINKER.   What a name! Tell me, what's this Careen like?

PAUL.   She loves rococo art. Homemade knödles
                and beer for dinner.

GRINKER.   Ha ha ha! Sounds nice!

PAUL.   Her father is this German bureau chief,
               and one time she was sitting on his lap
               in front of me, smiling, with her bare arm
               up around his neck, like this. She's the one
               who needs some therapy, don't you think? She flashed
               her tits at me once down this long hallway
               in her father's condo—I don't know why
               I feel the need to keep talking about
               her father. She's blonde. Great body. Sexy
               voice. Calls me Paulie. She doesn't let me
               have sex with her though. We share a house but
               I pay the rent. I live in a closet
               -sized room off the kitchen. I'm happiest
               on her leash, so to speak. I like to sit
               with her when she takes a bath or lying
               in bed with candles lit, drinking wine or
               smoking a joint, while she gets herself off
               beneath the covers. It's not sex, she says.
               It's only for comfort, Paulie. She likes
               to tell me that. One time she let this guy
               into our yard to watch through the window
               while she fucked this other guy. She described
               this at breakfast, in great detail. She wants
               to be a war reporter, so we went
               to Rwanda where we met this handsome
               aid worker named Laurent. Who was building
               latrines for refugees. And there I was
               with my camera in my one hand. Shooting
               pictures. By that evening she was lying
               in his tent, under his netting, writing
               in her diary. He got a hotel room
               underneath ours. With grenades exploding

in the shanties and the death squads spreading
through the streets, I call downstairs. She answers
laughing,

KHAREEN.   Paulie?

PAUL.   We have to go.

KHAREEN.   Not now,
Laurent.

PAUL.   They're killing people outside.

KHAREEN.   Get
off me please, Laurent!

PAUL.   He's living with us
here in Johannesburg. They fight and then fuck
all the time.

GRINKER.   Why don't we stop for the day.
I'm going to write you a prescription for
450 milligrams of
moclobemide.

PAUL.   Okay. Is that good?

GRINKER.   No,
that is bad. You're clinically depressed and
you have post-traumatic stress disorder.
It's good that you've come. Do you have someone
at home? Besides that sick woman, of course.
These drugs will take some time to change your brain
chemistry, and we don't want you killing
yourself in the meanwhile.

PAUL.   —Do you believe
in ghosts, Dr. Grinker?

GRINKER.   Well, I believe
people are haunted.

PAUL.   What if I told you
I came to you in the first place because
I'm haunted. Cursed.

GRINKER.   I'd ask you some questions
to rule out schizophrenia.

PAUL.   I told him
about the picture.

GRINKER.   It's famous. It's yours?

PAUL.   Then I told him what Cleveland's voice told me.

CLEVELAND. If you do this,

CLEVELAND.   I'll own you forever.

GRINKER.   That was your superego. Your mind was
simply speaking to itself.

PAUL.   I know what
my own mind sounds like. This was somebody
else.

GRINKER.   The soldier?

PAUL.   I've felt him next to me,
feared his presence.

GRINKER.   Is he here with us now?

PAUL.   He is. He's here when I wake up, he's there
when I'm asleep. He's with me whenever
I'm happy, when I'm having fun or sex
or watching TV, as if he's saying,
This can not last. And of course he's with me
whenever things go wrong. He's happiest
when I'm in pain. He'll never go away
till he gets what he wants from me.

GRINKER.   And what
does he want from you, Paul?

6: Iraq

PAUL.   This was in Mosul in Northern Iraq
at the beginning of the war. A boy
was throwing some pebbles at a marine

humvee, whose .50 caliber machine gun
was whipping and twisting like a fire hose
spraying death. And as I'm taking pictures
a gang of students comes rushing by with
another student bleeding from a deep
gash in his face. Somebody makes that sound,
you know, *click*, like, Take his picture! And while
I'm switching lenses you can see the switch
go on in somebody's head. Like, He's white,
what the hell's he doing here? I'm lifted
off the ground, tossed around, stoned. Somebody
slides his knife in my back and I'm feeling
the blood pooling in my shirt. I'm holding
onto my camera while they're stretching out
my arms, like this, till I'm floating on top
of the mob. And I'm not trying to be
cinematic here, but it was like Christ
on the cross. Cause I had absolutely
no sense of wanting to live. Or fighting
back. Protesting my innocence. Crying
out for mercy. I had this sense of, Well
we knew this was coming. And here it is.
But the truth of these places is always
the same. A dozen people, a dozen
against a multitude, formed a circle
around me. And we were close to this row
of shops that were closing, and these people
simply pulled the shutters up and shoved me
under. That's when I realize my camera's
gone, the hand's empty, the mob is pounding
on metal. The tea shop owner says, Look
you know I'd really like to help you but
would you mind leaving my tea shop soon? So

I end up in the street again kneeling
in the dirt at the order of some pissed
-off marines, and somehow I convince them
to take me back behind the wire. That's why
I know it's not just my brain, Doctor. Or
my father dying when I was two. Or
this hand. It would be poetic justice to
get ripped apart by a mob. Remember
what Cleveland said to me: If you do this
I will own you. I just have this feeling
he's thinking, You watched my desecration,
now here comes yours.

7: Some Embarrassing Things. Or, The Plan

DAN.   Dear Paul. It's been a while. Apologies.
           I've finally escaped from the Wisconsin
           winter, and I'm back in my strange new home,
           LA. I've just filled my prescription for
           Zoloft. And I'm hoping you're still willing
           to write this play, or whatever it is,   [*Google map:*
           with me. I know it's been a long time since   *Los Angeles.*]
           I first reached out to you. Maybe sometime
           I could give you a call?

PAUL.   I have to go
           to the Philippines, where Abu Sayyaf
           the local Al-Qaeda affiliate
           is on the march once again. I'm worried
           my editor, who hates me for reasons
           I can't even pretend to comprehend,
           won't like it. It's not the sort of story
           that tends to garner those coveted clicks
           on the *Times'* website.

DAN.   It's 75
degrees here and sunny. Women's faces
are slick masks, thanks to Botox. Some men look
embalmed and tan also. I walk my dog
four times a day. The only helicopters
I see here are LAPD circling
over Brentwood like they're still looking for
OJ's white Bronco. While I'm running up
Amalfi to Sunset the Palisades
look more like the hills of South Korea
on *MASH*. Or Tuscany. Where are you now,
Paul? What's your cell number? Can I call you?
Can I come visit you in Jakarta
soon?

PAUL.   I thought you might enjoy hearing this
sound bite directly from the fetid mouth
of our paper's new owner, Sam Zell. Here's
a link: http://gawker.com/
5002815/exclusive   *[Moving image,*
-sam-zell-says-fuck-you-to-his-journalist   *silent: http://*
                                                gawker.com/
ZELL.   My attitude on journalism is   *5002815/exclusive*
simple: I want to make enough money   *-sam-zell-says-fuck*
so I can afford you!   *-you-to-his-*
                                                 journalist]
PAUL.   And while it's true
I like a gutter-talking billionaire
as much as the next guy, I do wonder
what he's up to. Especially after
publishing a new employee manual
telling us all to question authority
and "push back."

ZELL.   I'm sorry, I'm sorry but
you're giving me the classic what I call
journalistic arrogance of deciding
that puppies don't count!

PAUL.   With all the chaos
building at the gates in Afghanistan
and Iraq, he's just the sort of leader
I'm not willing to die for.

ZELL.   Hopefully
we'll get to the point where our revenue
is so significant we'll be able
to do both puppies *and* Iraq. Okay?
—Fuck you!

PAUL.   So if ghostly voices ever
figure into this script, maybe this clip
will make a good one.

DAN.   Don't you think it's strange
you've never heard my voice, Paul? I've heard yours
on *All Things Considered,* the *LA Times'*
website. Let's set this trip up now! I won
a grant to come visit you.

PAUL.   Hey, congrats
on the grant! I've got a rusted RV
in Bali, we can watch the surf and drink
and discuss genocide. Only problem is
I finally got fired. And my RV
just got crushed by a tree. But have no fear!
I've got an idea.

DAN.   My wife's an actress
on a TV show that flopped. We're not sad
about it at all, but everyone thinks
we should be. It's winter, but it's sunny   *[Moving*
and warm. Every season's the same: sunny   *image:*
and warm. I have trouble remembering what   *water at*
season it is without thinking. The days   *mid-day.]*
get shorter or longer but the sun stays
the same. I go out running on the beach
at dusk. It's beautiful. It's beautiful.
It's beautiful.

PAUL.   I'm going to move back home
to Canada, where the plan is I'll work   *[Google*
for the *Toronto Star* again. Covering   *terrain*
the Arctic aboriginal beat. Shooting   *map:*
pictures, writing stories, blogging about   *Canadian*
life in the midnight sun. Or the noontime   *Arctic.]*
moon. In any case I've been waking up
thankful each morning I won't have to write
another sentence about Al-Qaeda
ever again. Unless Zawahiri's
hiding in some ice cave.

DAN.   You have no clue,
Paul, how happy this makes me! You have no
idea how much the ice-and-snow-and-wind
speaks to me, so much more so than the sun
of LA, or Bali. My entire life
I've been obsessed with nineteenth-century
polar exploration. Trapped in the ice
for months, sometimes years. Scurvy, insanity,
cannibalism. It helps me relax
and fall asleep. So maybe I could come
visit you there this winter? And who knows
maybe the Arctic will be the second
act of our play? Cause I have this deadline
coming up—

PAUL.   What kind of deadline?

DAN.   It's mine
and it's soon. The end of winter. So when
will you give me your God damned phone number
so I can plan this trip?

PAUL.   What are they like,
Dan?

DAN.   What?

PAUL.   Your plays.

DAN.   I don't know. Historical,
       like I said. I prefer things in books.

PAUL.   Why?

DAN.   I like things that have already happened
       to other people, a long time ago.

PAUL.   Why?

DAN.   I don't know. I have some ideas but—

PAUL.   Like what?

DAN.   Well the truth is I'm insecure
       around you, Paul. You intimidate me
       terribly. You're like this mythic figure,
       with your hand, your constant returning to
       the underworld of the most nauseating
       things in history. Recent history. You've looked
       at that which the rest of us won't look at,
       or can't look at. You're the type of writer
       I've always wished I were. Engaged with life,
       people.

PAUL.   You don't engage much with people?

DAN.   No. I like to seclude myself. Like you
       I like to stay away. Sometimes I lay
       my head against my dog's head and I think,
       You're my best friend. You're my only friend. If
       you get sick I'll get a second mortgage
       for you. Even though we don't have a first
       mortgage yet. We're just renters. I even
       like my obsessions but I don't know why
       I do. Like I said, I have my theories
       but I think they'd be boring to someone
       like you.

PAUL.   ·   Try me.

DAN.   I'm like you, like I said.
       Like you I'll sometimes cry for no reason
       at all. Or I don't cry for months and months

and months. Like you I see flashbacks. I'm scared
to change that part of me that's craziest,
because if I'm not crazy anymore
how will I do what I do? I'm the same
age you were in Mogadishu, the same
age Sgt. Cleveland was that day. I'm cursed
too, just like you are.

PAUL.   But you won't tell me
what's cursing you?

DAN.   Because it can't compare
to what you've been through!

PAUL.   After my memoir
came out, I'd hear from strangers who'd tell me
the most intimate things about themselves.
Embarrassing. About their lives. They saw
that just like them I had these internal
conflicts. Except you, you didn't confess
anything. Which is probably why I wrote
you back. Do you know that quote of Camus'
where he says he's solved the mystery of where
war lives? It lives in each of us, he said.
In the loneliness and humiliation
we all feel. If we can solve that conflict
within ourselves then we'll be able to
rid the world of war. Maybe. So tell me,
Dan: where does war live in you?

DAN.   My family
stopped talking to me, several years ago,
and I have no idea why. That's not true,
I have many ideas but none of them
make sense. I was about to get married
but it wasn't like they didn't approve
of my wife. It had something to do with

the fact that nobody would be coming
from my family because they have no friends.
I mean literally my parents don't have
any friends. They can barely leave the house
and whatever's left of their own families
won't speak to them for reasons I've never
understood. And I'd just written a play
that was the closest I'd come to writing
autobiography. And my brother
was in the hospital again, for God
knows what exactly, depression mostly.
He hadn't spoken to any of us
in years. Which was mostly okay with me
cause like everyone else in my family
I suppose I just wanted to forget
he'd ever existed at all. Maybe
this was all because of him? reminding
my family of what happened years ago
when I was 12 and he was 17,   *[Moving image:*
one Tuesday afternoon in February   *snow falling.]*
walking up the driveway when I noticed
him coming around the house with his back
all pressed with snow, the back of his head white
with snow, and I thought it was so funny
he wasn't wearing a jacket or shoes.
He was barefoot. And by funny I mean
disturbing. I've told this story thousands
of times, I hardly feel a thing. He'd jumped
out of a window, was what I found out
later, and fallen three stories without
breaking a bone. That night my mother cried
in my arms and said, This is a secret
we will take to our graves. I developed

innumerable compulsions, including
counting, hand-washing, scrupulosity
which is the fear that one has been sinful
in word or deed or thought. I was afraid
to leave the house, to touch any surface,
but I hid it so well that nobody
noticed. I was class president. I played
baseball, soccer. I wrote secret poetry.
And eventually I got out and went
to college. And things went coasting along
as well as things can in a family with
an inexplicably cruel father and
a masochistic mother who can't stop
talking about nothing. Logorrhea
is the clinical term, I think. Until
I came home one weekend for a visit
just before my wedding and my father
said I looked homeless. My beard and hair. When
in fact I looked just like other adjunct
professors of writing. But they told me
I looked like a man who'd slit his own throat
soon. They said I looked just like my father's
brother, a man who disappeared after
I was born. He was tall, he was funny,
long hair and barefoot in jeans, a hippy
and some kind of artist. The opposite
of my father. I'm the spitting image
of this man, they said. They were terrified
for this reason. There are things you don't know!
my father kept saying, without saying
what it was exactly I didn't know.
My mother and father were both screaming
together, it felt almost sexual.

There are things you don't know! I drove away
and haven't heard from them since. They are dead
to me. And I don't mean that in the way
it sounds, melodramatically. I mean
I can't remember them. And by memory
I mean I can't feel. I have no pictures
of my childhood. It's like my entire life
up until I was 33 happened
to someone else. Someone who's haunting me,
who makes me feel cursed. Makes me feel certain
that yes, they're right, I've failed, something is wrong
with me. I don't know what it is but yes
something is wrong. I've failed, I've failed, I've failed,
I've failed. Only writing and running helps
some. I sit at my desk like a lab rat
clicking on a button that shows me who's
visiting my website. And it doesn't
tell me who's visiting exactly but
it shows your city or town on a map
of the entire world. When I said they don't
talk to me, that wasn't true. I can tell
my mother checks my website at least once
a day. Sometimes twice. It's a compulsion,
I know, but still I like seeing those dots
on the map. But it's nothing! it's nothing
to complain about, it's the sort of thing
everybody has. And nothing compared
to the unspeakable acts of cruelty
you've seen, Paul.

PAUL.   Let's get together somewhere
in the Upper Arctic, in 24
-hour darkness, this winter. The hotels there
are like dorms for racist construction crews

from the south, and the costs run high because
everything's flown in. But the ambience
will be just perfect. So let me know when
you'd like to come, and I'll put together
some kind of plan.

8: Hi What's Your Name When Are You Leaving?

DAN.   Sand snow sand snow sand snow sand snow sand snow
snow snow snow.

DAN.   LAX to Vancouver,
Vancouver to Yellowknife.   *[Google Earth:*
DAN.   What the hell   *Yellowknife,*
kind of name is Yellowknife? I've read that   *Northwest*
                                                  Territories,
DAN.   copper in the ground turned the Inuit's   *Canada.]*
knives yellow.

DAN.   Yellowknife to Kugluktuk   *[Google Earth:*
by twin turboprop. How do you say that   *Kugluktuk,*
name again?   *Northwest*
                                               Territories.]
DAN.   Kugluktuk. But I don't know
Inuktitut.

DAN.   What's that?

DAN.   Their language.

DAN.   Whose?

DAN.   The Inuit. Which means simply people
in Inuktitut.

DAN.   I'm getting all this
information off Wikipedia
on my new iPhone.

DAN.   The flight attendant
DAN.   is an Inuit kid, gay, goth, nose ring
and an attitude.

ATTENDANT.   Does anyone want

this last bottle of water?

DAN.   The pilots
are supposedly Inuit too, though
the cockpit door's closed the whole way. No one
speaks over the intercom. A black guy
dressed all in white shares the aisle with me:

BLACK GUY. What brings you to the North, my mon?

DAN.   His voice
sounds almost Jamaican.

BLACK GUY.   True dat, true dat.
Are you done with your paper, mon?

DAN.   Later
I'll find out his name's Isaac, from Ghana,
when Paul's interviewing him.

DAN.   His family
immigrated to Yellowknife after
some coup in the '80s.

DAN.   An old woman
in traditional clothes, like calico
fringed with coyote fur, her hood hiding
her face,

DAN.   doesn't say a word.

DAN.   A teenaged
girl with an iPod as we're descending
into Kugluktuk

DAN.   taps me on the arm

DAN.   and asks me, smiling wide,

INUIT GIRL.   Hi what's your name
when are you leaving?

DAN.   Grandma and the girl
shuffling across the ice of Kugluktuk
while Isaac and I fly two more hours north   *[Google Earth:*
to Ulukhaktok.   *Ulukhaktok.]*

DAN.   Where the airport is
                    a room,
DAN.   the cab's a van gliding across
                    a desert of snow.
DAN.   Sand snow.
DAN.   The cabbie's
                    white, from Newfoundland, a newfy.
DAN.   Which means
                    he's some kind of Canadian redneck,
DAN.   according to Wikipedia.
TAXI DRIVER.   Why
                    don't you drive the taxi eh? Joe asks me.
                    You know where everyone lives. Everyone
                    lives in the same flipping place!
DAN.   Then he asks
                    Isaac, probably because he's black:
TAXI DRIVER.   Are you
                    here to teach basketball eh?
ISAAC.   No, soccer.
TAXI DRIVER. That'll be ten dollars eh.
ISAAC.   I got it, I got it
                    —welcome to the North, my mon!
DAN.   The hotel's
                    a prefab one-story house, corrugated
                    tin roof, windows for like six rooms.
DAN.   Inside   *[Image:*
                    it smells like Clorox. Inuit women   *hallway of*
                    scrubbing the deep fryer.   *hotel in*
                                                            Ulukhaktok.]
INUIT WOMAN.   Hi what's your name
                    when are you leaving?
DAN.   I'm filling out forms
                    at the front desk, which is just a closet
                    with a desk inside it. Paul had emailed

we might have to share a room. Please God don't
make us share a room. What if he tries to
get in bed with me? What if he kills me
in my sleep? in his sleep? What happens if
he hangs himself in our shower? At least
then I'll have my second act.

PAUL.   Are you Dan?
I'm Paul.

DAN.   His hair's messed up. He needs a shave.
His thick wool socks are sloughing off.

DAN.   Pink eyes,
unfocused.

DAN.   There's a deep crease in his face,
between his eyes like it's carved.

DAN.   He's wearing
an old sweatshirt with a red maple leaf
on it.

DAN.   Who does this man remind me of?

DAN.   He's somebody I should know.

DAN.   Paul's left hand
is a stub. Like his arm simply runs out
of arm. But he's still got some kind of thumb
at the end. He's rubbing his furrowed brow
with it.

PAUL.   How was Eskimo Air?

DAN.   Don't look,
Dan.

DAN.   Not now.

DAN.   Show what kind of man you are

DAN.   by not looking at Paul's hand.

DAN.   I wonder
what I look like to him?

PAUL.   You look a lot
              like Jesus. You know that?

DAN.   Thanks?

PAUL.   You're a real
              tight packer. Wow.

DAN.   I brought dehydrated
              food. You wrote me the food sucked so I bought
              dehydrated organic lasagna
              at REI in Santa Monica?

PAUL.   Ooh, I love that stuff!

DAN.   Let me just finish
              with this form, and I'll swing by your room.

PAUL.   Our
              room. Door's always open.

DAN.   —Hey!

PAUL.   Come on in
              Dan, have a seat.   *[Moving image:*

DAN.   So.   *gently snowing*

PAUL.   So.   *window.]*

DAN.   So here we are
              finally!

PAUL.   Finally! I know it's not that much
              to look at. But these beds are pretty firm.
              They keep the heat so high you'll want to sleep
              on top of the blankets, but it's better
              than bunking in here with some drunk racist
              construction worker from Edmonton, right?

DAN.   Right!

PAUL.   And cell phones don't work. But the wireless
              is free. In case you want to Skype your wife.
              I Skype my wife pretty much every night,
              if you know what I mean. Ha ha ha. —So
              what do you want to do this week? Because

we never really decided, only
that you'd come.

DAN. And watch you work.

PAUL. And watch me
interview people. You're going to get bored.

DAN. I could interview you. You know, research
for the play. If you want.

INUIT GIRLS. Hi what's your name
when are you leaving?

DAN. Two Inuit girls
appear in the doorway. Like *The Shining*
or something. Selling key chains and lanyards
made of sealskin.

PAUL. Not now. Go away.

DAN. Why
are they all asking that, Hi what's your name
when are you leaving?

PAUL. They're just assuming
we're leaving soon. Like every other white
person they've ever met.

DAN. I wish I had
my recorder.

PAUL. You lost it?

DAN. I left it
on the plane.

PAUL. You can borrow mine. Here. Catch.
I used it for years in Afghanistan
and Iraq.

DAN. How's it turn on?

PAUL. The batteries
are dead. You could probably buy some new ones
at the cantina. Or just remember
all my wise words, ha ha ha.

DAN.   Do you miss   [Image:
        Afghanistan, Paul? places like that?   bright light.]

DAN.   Sand
        snow snow.

DAN.   Do you feel you've made a mistake
        leaving war reporting behind? It's like
        you've been sent away to Siberia
        literally. Or is it like a respite?
        a reward for everything before?

DAN.   But
        I don't ask him any of that. Instead
        I ask:

DAN.   Do you ever get bored up here,
        Paul? It must get kind of lonely.

PAUL.   That's right,
        but I learn a lot of things too.

DAN.   Like what?

PAUL.   Like you shouldn't ask too many questions
        about polar bear hunts, for example.
        It's shamanistic. The Inuit still
        believe shamans can turn themselves into
        spirits, into animals like muskox
        and seals and bears. That shamans can
        become other people too. All in the pursuit
        of exorcising ghosts—   [Moving image:

DAN.   Should I tell him   falling snow]
        that for weeks I've been having this feeling
        when I run that somebody is running
        with me?

DAN.   Sand sand sand.

DAN.   Over my shoulder
        in the sun and the sand.

DAN.   Who is that man
who's running after me?

DAN.   Which reminds me
of that story of Ernest Shackleton
down at the opposite pole, staggering
through a blizzard with his fellow travelers
starving, delirious,

DAN.   how they kept seeing
someone with them.

DAN.   how they kept asking,

DAN.   Who
is that man who walks always beside you?

DAN.   Is Staff Sgt. William David Cleveland
following me? And what could he possibly
want from me? I don't say any of this
to Paul.

DAN.   Snow snow.

DAN.   I don't want him thinking
I'm too crazy.

PAUL.   Hey, want to watch TV?

DAN.   We could try to track down a shaman.

PAUL.   Who?

DAN.   That's something we could do. This week. Maybe
he could try to heal you. Ha ha ha.

PAUL.   Oh   [Sound:
that reminds me: I'm trying to set up   dogs howling
this dog sled ride with these two Inuit   far away,
hunters named Jack and Jerry. 500   chains, wind.]
dollars but I'll pay them, the *Toronto
Star* will I mean. Do you hear those huskies
howling? They're chained on the ice all their lives.
I don't know how they take it, the boredom
I mean. Because you're right, there's definitely

a lot of boredom up here. It's supposed
to snow tomorrow, but we'll go sledding
if the weather's any good.

*[Moving image:
more snow
falling,
becoming
a blizzard
of white.]*

9: Blizzard

Where's the remote? Do you like John Mayer?
I like John Mayer. And Ryan Adams
too. And Queen Latifah. I like to watch
TV with the sound off and just listen
to my iTunes. This okay with you? This
sucks. This sucks. There's nothing good on TV!
I usually watch just like sports, hockey
and football, sometimes entertainment news
because it's stupid but I love it when
celebrities do stupid things. It helps
me relax. And I like watching curling
as an Olympic sport. I love hearing
the women's curling team screaming, Harder!
Faster! All of these women with their brooms
that look more like Swiffer WetJets rubbing
some kind of path in the ice for the weight
or the pot or the stone or whatever
screaming, Harder! Faster! As if that does
anything, really! What about this show,
The Bachelor? Have you seen *The Bachelor?* Look,
she's pretending to cry. She's pretending
to cry! What are all these people, actors?
Strippers? She's trying so damn hard to cry
real tears! Harder! Faster! How's it look?

*[Light: dark
Arctic noon.]*

*[Moving image:
window full of
snow.]*

*[Sound:
Ryan Adams
singing
"Rescue Blues"
low.]*

DAN.   Looks
bad.

PAUL.   It must be gusting up to like, what,

65 an hour?

DAN.   My iPhone says that
it's negative 50 out there.

PAUL.   Wind chill
included?

DAN.   I'm not sure, let's see.

PAUL.   Celsius
or Fahrenheit?

DAN.   I'm Googling it.

PAUL.   I think
Celsius and Fahrenheit become the same
at minus 40 anyway.

DAN.   Earlier
Jack the Inuit hunter woke us up
with some coffee.   *[Light: dark dawn.]*

JACK.   Morning, Paul. Morning, Dan.
Looking really bad out there.

DAN.   Almost ten
and it's basically sunrise.

JACK.   The next time
you come up here you bring me a brand new
skidoo. Okay? Maybe helicopter.

DAN.   Before the ban on polar bear hunting
businessmen from Texas would come up here
and Jack would help them track down a mother
bear to shoot. And mount. These rich guys would leave
enormous tips, like snowmobiles.

JACK.   Bad news:
can't go out sledding this morning. Jerry's
got the dogs and Jerry's at the doctor's
because he's got like this titanium plate?
in his forehead, from a real bad sled crash
few years back. Ha ha ha. And anyway

Elder says this snow's no good. GPS
can't see shit today. We'll go tomorrow
at nine, Inuit time.

DAN.   Inuit time   *[Light: mid-*
means what, Paul?   *afternoon.*

PAUL.   At least we've got the wi-fi,   *Back to the*
and this six-pack of Bordeaux I picked up   *soundless*
in Yellowknife.   *TV screen.]*

DAN.   I didn't bring any
alcohol. How could I forget to buy
alcohol?

PAUL.   You're not bored are you?   *[Laptop*
DAN.   I was   *playing*
hoping at some point we might get back to   *music, John*
interviewing you?   *Mayer,*

PAUL.   I'm an open book,   *"Stop This*
Dan. Blank slate. No secrets.   *Train*
                                                 (Acoustic)
DAN.   You want to read   *(Live).]*
our play? I've got a first act but—

PAUL.   I can't
figure out my story. Global warming
or the arts. Or corruption. There's something
shady going on here, I can feel it
with the white guys running this place. Kickbacks
or something. Maybe it's better not to
stir things up too much? don't want to end up
dead in a snowdrift, right?

DAN.   Paul's popping pills
out of his many-chambered plastic pill
organizer—

PAUL.   Depression, blood pressure,
Polycystic Kidney—

DAN.   Which reminds me

to take my Zoloft.

PAUL. Oh God I love this *[Light: evening.]*
movie.

DAN. That evening it's *The River Wild.*

PAUL. Meryl Streep's on the run, on the river *[Laptop plays*
actually ha ha ha, in a rafting *Queen Latifah's*
boat trying to escape from this psycho *"Lush Life"*
-killer Kevin Bacon. Is this movie *low.]*
good? or shit. It's shit but Jesus Meryl
Streep is so gorgeous.

DAN. Paul, can I ask you
some questions, maybe during commercial
breaks?

PAUL. Sure. Shoot.

DAN. I'm thinking it would help me
finish our play. Which you're welcome to read
at any point, by the way—

PAUL. Do you want
a glass of Bordeaux?

DAN. Yes please.

PAUL. Go ahead.
Blank book, open slate.

DAN. What is it about
the Arctic—?

PAUL. I guess I'm just happiest
when I'm unhappy. When I'm on the phone
with one of my brothers and he's talking
about, you know, problems at work. I say,
How long we been talking? 15 minutes.
I say: Now you're 15 minutes closer
to death.

DAN. I'm sure he loves that.

PAUL.   It bugs me
          to the core though! that people don't notice
          how quickly we die. Whether you're driving
          home from work, or suntanning on a beach
          in Phuket and this wave comes in and just
          keeps on coming—

DAN.   How can you live like that?
          I mean, how can you walk around living
          like you're going to die? Like back in LA
          you can't be worried about the earthquake
          that could erupt any second. You can't
          ride the New York City subway thinking
          about the likelihood of a terrorist
          bomb exploding. Like on 9/11
          I woke up—

PAUL.   You were there?

DAN.   And actually
          I saw a ghost in our bedroom. Covered in
          dust. Carrying his briefcase. He looked
          so confused! He disappeared and I heard
          the sirens. I went downstairs to find out
          what was going on, and to hit Starbuck's
          too. All these papers were spiraling down
          from the sky. And I remember thinking
          for a minute, Now all the bankers will
          be humbled. I got my venti latte
          and came back out in time to see the plane
          hit the second tower. An old woman
          sat down on the pavement and just started
          sobbing. I went upstairs to get my wife
          though we weren't married yet, and we joined
          a river of people like refugees
          walking uptown. While all the working men

and women were jumping. I never saw
my brother jumping out of the window
of our house, all those years ago. Maybe
there's something in that? A radio outside
a hardware store in Chinatown told us
the South Tower had come down. In a bar
somewhere in the East Village we watched as
the North Tower sank out of the blue sky
on TV. People were almost giddy
with panic, and grief. Some guys were tossing
a Frisbee in the street. I told myself,
If there's going to be a war, I will go.
I saw myself holding a machine gun
in my mind's eye, someplace bright and sandy
like Afghanistan, or maybe Iraq.
But I didn't go. Because I didn't
consider it the right war. Or because
nobody made me.

PAUL.   And are you hoping
I'll forgive you?

DAN.   My point is maybe not
everyone's meant to be as courageous
as you are.

PAUL.   It's not courage—

DAN.   It's also
altruistic. Necessary. If you
don't do what you do then none of us will
ever have any idea what's really
going on.

PAUL.   When I started out it was
all for self-esteem. I'm sure you started
out the same way too. I wanted people
to say I was brave, and heroic. Then

I began to hate it but I needed
that fix of adrenalin. The third stage,
where I am now? I don't really need it
anymore. But now I see the lies, now
I see how the people doing my job
don't get it. Or if they get it they don't
talk about it. They want success, they want
a seat at the Sunday morning talk show
round table. They want their own cable show.
I just want to chip away at those lies
now. But that's a losing game. Most people
don't care what's going on, or they don't know
what they're supposed to do. So we just stop
listening to the litany of evidence
of the coups we're pulling off, the phosphorus
bombs dropping on Fallujah in '04
that melted the skin off children—I could
go on and on and on and on. That's why
I object to the word altruistic.

DAN.   Why? Because you're too angry?

PAUL.   I see it
as a labyrinth: if you can find the truth
you get out. But you don't, it just gets worse,
you get more lost. And the harder you try
the darker it gets. As opposed to what,
being like you, I guess. Right, Dan? Who cares?
Let's watch some more TV. Let's drink more wine.
As long as I'm safe I don't need to do
a thing!

DAN.   I guess that's fair.

PAUL.   Sorry. See? This
is why I don't like to talk to people

besides my wife. People ask me questions
they don't want the answers to.

DAN. Do you want
to unmute the movie?

JACK. Morning, Paul. Dan,
the next time you come up here from LA
you bring me back a black twenty-year-old
girl. Okay? *[Light: dim sunrise.]*

DAN. Next morning Jack says maybe
we'll go out on the land. Till an elder
stands up and peers out the kitchen window
at the snowflakes floating in a milky
morning light.

JACK. Elder says,

ELDER. Earth is moving
faster now. *[Moving*

JACK. He means this weather's messed up *image:*
cause of climate change. Says we'd better wait *blizzard in*
until tomorrow. *the window.]*

DAN. The snow is moving
faster now, I can't tell if it's falling
out of the sky or up from the treeless
lunarscape. —Jack, do you happen to know
any shamans around here?

PAUL. Dan's thinking
it'll make a good story.

DAN. It might be,
I don't know, entertaining.

JACK. A shaman?

DAN. You know, a medicine man. A healer
of some kind?

JACK. Sure. Roger.

DAN. Roger?

JACK. Roger

Umtoq. He's a storyteller? Makes stone
sculptures, junk like that. He lives out beyond
the trap lines in Minto Inlet. Don't know
if he's still alive.

DAN.   Could you ask around
for his number? or email?

PAUL.   Jack told me   *[Light: evening.*
last winter one of these blizzards lasted   *Moving image:*
fourteen days.   *blizzard in*
                                                     the window.]

DAN.   Fourteen days!

PAUL.   That's a fortnight
to Canadians.

DAN.   Later that evening
we're getting into bed, snow is whispering
beneath the windowpanes.

PAUL.   I wouldn't mind
staying here for a while. Just between me
and you, my confessor. They're refusing
to send me anywhere interesting
these days. I don't know why.

DAN.   Are you afraid
you'll be fired?

PAUL.   Of course. Nobody's reading
anything anymore. Are you?

DAN.   Reading
newspapers?

PAUL.   And nobody's clicking on
these Arctic pieces either. My expense
reports are obscene.

DAN.   Why not do something
else then?

PAUL.   Like what? Maybe I could become
a wedding photographer.

DAN.   Why don't you

write a book?

PAUL.   I already wrote a book.
Remember? I think I sold like maybe
six copies in the US. One review
on Amazon said:

AMAZON.   The lesson we learn,
that war lives in all of us, is neither
original nor particularly
helpful.

AMAZON.   Author Watson is at his best
whilst giving us the sights and sounds of war,

AMAZON.   but his memoir suffers when he aspires
to some kind of poetry whose only
loyalty is to the truth.

PAUL.   I'm paraphrasing
now, of course, but what kind of an ass-jag
uses the word whilst?

DAN.   Your book had no   *[Light: lights out.*
point for me actually. To be completely   *Sound: wind*
honest with you. I would read a chapter   *howling.]*
or two, then have to put it down. And go
wash my hands. Because—it was all too much!
And repetitive. All these horrible
things you've lived through, I still don't understand
how you don't just surrender to profound
despair.

PAUL.   Have I ever told you about
the time I met Mother Theresa?

DAN.   No.

PAUL.   I was stuck in Calcutta—

DAN.   I'm going to
record this, okay?

PAUL.   So I went over

to Mother's House. Which was this heavily
trafficked place, full of these shady-looking
characters wearing Rolex watches and
Italian business suits. There was a chair
by the door, and a sister said:

SISTER.   Sit down,
and if she's willing she will come.

PAUL.   Maybe
two or three days passed like this, till someone,
some sister comes downstairs and says,

SISTER.   Mother
will see you now.

SISTER.   Only for a short while,

SISTER.   a moment if you're lucky.

PAUL.   I turn on
my tape recorder and race up the stairs
where she's hobbling around in her knobby
crippled kind of bare feet in this small room
of hers with no doors,

PAUL.   just some curtains and
I'm watching her shuffle back and forth from

PAUL.   one doorway to the other,

PAUL.   appearing
and then disappearing in the sunlight
and then shade.

PAUL.   Never once looking at me.
Because I'd been to her treatment centers,
she didn't call them that, they're basically
places to go and die, right?

DAN.   Right.

PAUL.   Full of
row upon row of starving AIDS victims
and others,

PAUL.   lying on these sorts of cots very low to the ground.

PAUL.   And they don't get
a lot of medical care, they get cleaned
and they get fed.

PAUL.   They don't get fed a lot.

PAUL.   And I was trying to be this heavy
on Mother Theresa, you know, saying,
Don't you think you should feed them some more food?

PAUL.   Don't you think maybe you should be doing
this or that?

PAUL.   And she said, They don't need food.
They need love. And she kept on saying that.

MOTHER.   They need love. They need love. That's all. That's all.

PAUL.   I was thinking, Wow, this is like shooting
ducks in a pond! This woman's a moron,
right?

DAN.   Ha ha ha, right!

PAUL.   So I go and write
my hit-piece about Mother Theresa.
It wasn't this blatant, but basically
what I said was that she was this harpy,
this, you know, cold-hearted nun mistreating
all these poor people. Well—bullshit. She's right.
What they *did* need was love. Because it was
respect. Either they die in the street or
they die in Mother's House. And if you die
in Mother's arms then at least you've died with
somebody loving you. And not because
they owe it to you, or because they feel
some familial obligation—they're just
doing it because they know you deserve
to be loved. You know? Maybe I'm a fool
but I think that was the point of my book
that no one bought.

DAN.   So what you're saying is

war would disappear if we could all just
hold each others' hands?

PAUL.   Why are you trying
to turn me into some kind of guru?

DAN.   Am I?

PAUL.   Like I've got some kind of answer
for you.

DAN.   I don't know.

PAUL.   That thing you wrote me
about your family, Dan. They disowned you
for no reason.

DAN.   Right.

PAUL.   And how your father
kept saying, There are things you do not know!
And how you look just like your dad's brother,
I keep thinking about that.

DAN.   I do too.

PAUL.   Did your father mean he's not your father?

DAN.   I don't know. It's crazy, but—

PAUL.   Why don't you
start asking some questions? That's what I'd do
if I were you.

DAN.   Paul's laptop starts ringing.

PAUL.   It's Skype. It's my wife. Stay here.

DAN.   No I'll go
sit in the kitchen.

PAUL.   No stay here. Hello?
Sweetness?

DAN.   I hear Paul's wife's voice. I don't look
at the screen. I go out to the hallway
and sit by the pay phone. And try calling
home on an empty calling card.

PAUL.   Sweetness,

I miss you so badly.

DAN. The next morning *[Light: dawn,*
things look different. *no storm.]*

JACK. Next time you come up here,
Dan, you bring me back a bag of cocaine
and an AK-47.

DAN. We step
outside.

DAN. Snow snow.

DAN. Jerry's down on the ice
with his sled and his dog team. The sky is
bright, snow's drifting like pollen.

PAUL. Would you mind
riding with Jerry, Dan? Jack can pull me
behind his skidoo and I can shoot you
and the dogs that way.

DAN. Jerry's middle-aged
and mildly hunchbacked. I think I can see
that titanium plate in his forehead.

JERRY. Guys!
Guys! We're losing our sunlight here!

DAN. I snap
some pictures before my camera's frozen.

PAUL. Put it inside your coat! Put it next to
your skin!

DAN. I can't hear you!

JERRY. Hoot, hoot! *[Moving image:*

DAN. Jerry's *no sound*
beating his dogs' muzzles with a short stick. *Dan's footage*

JERRY. No, Ghost! Bad Ghost! *of the dogs.]*

DAN. You call your dog Ghost? Why?

JERRY. I'm training him to lead. I had to sell
my old leader. But Ghost's a real scaredy

-cat.

DAN.   The dogs are tangled in harnesses
of yellow nylon cords.

JERRY.   Misty wants to
lead instead.

DAN.   Who's Misty?

JERRY.   The one in back.

DAN.   She's cute. Smelly. Hyper. A bit dangerous.

JERRY.   Real bitch.

DAN.   They can't stop barking.

JERRY.   Hoot! Hoot!

DAN.   High
-pitched yelps. They seem insane. Like a savage
race of idiot wolves.

JERRY.   Hoot! Hoot!

DAN.   I'm missing
my dog now. She's a miniature schnauzer
these huskies would eat for breakfast. A few
of them are eating their own shit. Tearing
at hunks of meat.

JERRY.   Hoot! Hoot, hoot!

DAN.   Who knows what
Jerry's trying to say?

JERRY.   Sit your ass down,
Dan! —Hoot, hoot, hoot!

DAN.   And we're off. I'm sitting
down, on my ass, on a blue plastic tarp
with my rubber boots splayed in front, inches
above the ice above the sea—

JERRY.   Hold on
to these ropes down here, Dan!

DAN.   Jerry's kneeling
behind my ear.

JERRY.   Gee! Gee! Zaw!

DAN.   Gee means right,
I think. I've heard mushers say Haw! for left
but Jerry says

JERRY.   Zaw! —Hoot!

DAN.   means faster. Paul's
riding in a box on skis.

DAN.   Jack's pulling
him with his skidoo.

DAN.   Red taillights dancing
in a whorl of snow.

JERRY.   Hoot, hoot!

DAN.   You feel it
in your spine, your neck, your skull. The grinding
of the rusted runners on ice crystals   *[Moving image, silent*
like sand.   *this dog sled ride*

DAN.   Snow snow snow snow snow snow   *Dan's POV.]*

DAN.   Cresting
another invisible ridge, the dogs
fan out to shit in streaks.

JERRY.   Misty, no! Gee!
Gee!

DAN.   We're moving onto the Arctic Sea,
and if we could only change direction
and head that way—

JERRY.   Zaw! Zaw! Zaw!

DAN.   If we could
only get the dogs to turn to the left
instead,

DAN.   we'd be in Minto Inlet.

DAN.   Where
Roger Umtoq the shaman lives.

JERRY.   Misty,

no! —Zaw!

DAN.   We stop at the floe's edge. The sea
is an undulating eternity
of black slush a few feet away. Seal heads
breaking through the new ice, their spectral eyes
on us.

PAUL.   My feet are completely numb, Dan.

DAN.   I think I bruised my tailbone.

JERRY.   Hey guys! Guys!   *[More*
These dogs aren't tired enough yet! Got to   *footage*
keep going!   *no sound:*
                                                   dogs barking in
DAN.   The dogs keep barking,   *harness*

DAN.   while Paul   *on the*
sets up his tripod and shoots Jack kneeling   *ice.]*
at the waterline.

DAN.   tossing a snowball
onto the thin veneer of ice forming
on the water. It sounds like a pebble
bouncing off glass.

PAUL.   Have you ever seen it
this melted before?

JACK.   Usually ice floes
come down from the hill, usually springtime
like April May June?

JERRY.   Hey guys! Guys! These dogs
are real worked up! Going to have to run them
some more!

JACK.   Cause that's when we get the winds?
But I've never seen it this warm before
in wintertime.

JERRY.   Hey Dan.

DAN.   Yeah.

JERRY. Put your weight
on this anchor.

DAN. What for?

JERRY. Just stand on this
and don't go anywhere. I need to go
drain my dragon.

DAN. The anchor's a steel claw
dug in the ice. Tied with a yellow cord
that's tied to the very last barking dog
in the team. Named Misty.

JERRY. Misty! shut up!

DAN. Jerry!

JERRY. Huh?

DAN. Do you know Roger Umtoq
the shaman in Minto Inlet?

JERRY. Old guy?
Told kids bullshit stories?

DAN. He's a healer
too.

JERRY. I don't know nothing about all that.

DAN. Can you take us out to Minto Inlet
to see him? Of course we'll pay you something,
Jerry.

JERRY. I'd like to take you to Minto
but the Roger I know out in Minto
died of heart attack last winter—

DAN. Misty
takes off,

JERRY. Misty no!

DAN. pulling the whole team,

DAN. and the sled starts sliding sideways,

DAN. I start
laughing, like I'm embarrassed,

DAN.   as my boot
        slips off the anchor,

DAN.   as the anchor slips
        out of the ice—

JERRY.   What are you doing, Dan!

DAN.   Me?

JERRY.   Ghost! Ghost!

DAN.   And for an instant I see
        the top of the world from above,

PAUL.   Hey Dan,
        are you okay?

DAN.   as the steel anchor wraps
        around my ankle and whips me up off
        my feet,

PAUL.   I'm so sorry.

DAN.   and the seal heads   *[Light: Arctic*
        duck back under the new ice.   *night.]*

PAUL.   I'm feeling
        so guilty.

DAN.   We're back in our hotel room
        and I can't move.

PAUL.   How's your head?

DAN.   It's all right.

PAUL.   Do you need any more ice?

DAN.   It's my groin   *[TV on, no sound:*
        that's killing me.   *entertainment*

PAUL.   We're out of wine. You sure   *news.]*
        you didn't bring anything?

DAN.   I forgot,
        I told you. I'm sorry.

PAUL.   —You should've seen
        yourself, you were sideways! You were almost
        inverted! I don't know how that happened,

the physics of it, I mean. You don't have
anything to drink? no vodka?

DAN.   I wish
I had some right now.

PAUL.   This reminds me of
Abdul Haq—you know who he is right?

DAN.   No.

PAUL. He was this mujahedeen famous for
defeating the Soviets in the '80s
with the CIA's help, of course. After
9/11, I went to interview
him in Peshawar.

DAN.   Pakistan?

PAUL.   —Here here here
record this.

DAN.   Okay.

PAUL.   I mean this guy looked
exactly like Rob Reiner with a tan!
and a bright white shalwar kameez. He hugged
me! without knowing me! He was limping
around on his prosthetic foot. I'm sure
that's why he liked me.

DAN.   Why?

PAUL.   He was going
back to Kabul so that when the US
invaded he'd be an alternative
to the Taliban. I'm sure he wanted
revenge also, cause Talibs killed his wife
and son a few years before, or maybe
it was ISI—

DAN.   ISI is what
again, Paul?

PAUL.   I was eating and sleeping
on the floor, outside Kabul. With dried blood
in the corner, bullet holes in the wall.
Bathing in a bucket, with one toilet
all plugged up with shit. Everybody there
had dysentery. And somebody asked me,
Have you heard what happened to Abdul Haq?
He came over the Khyber Pass last week
with 25 men, and Taliban troops
ambushed him. He hid all night in the rocks
calling the CIA for air support
but no one came. Taliban captured him
the next morning and hanged him from a tree
with a metal noose. Cut off his dick and
stuffed it in his mouth. Shot up his body
till he was just this hanging piece of meat.
I'm sorry, Dan. Sorry. I don't know why
I'm thinking of him now. I don't know why
I'm crying either! Maybe it's just cause
you got tangled up in all that cord?

DAN.   Paul's
staying straight ahead. He's not here. Paul's not   *[Moving*
here anymore. I get up, head spinning,   *image:*
groin aching.   *snow*
                                                                          falling.]
PAUL.   Sorry, Dan. Sorry.

DAN.   I see
who he is now, finally: sitting there
in his socks, his filthy sweatshirt, his eyes
are like looking down a well. His greasy
hair's all messed up. He's my older brother
sitting at the kitchen table, the day
they brought him back home from the hospital.
I was standing in the doorway watching

him pretend to eat something. Nobody
was saying a word. I could have sat down
with him. I was scared I'd catch his disease.
I thought, Sadness is an illness you catch
if you aren't careful enough. I ran
outside to play with friends. Are you hungry,
Paul? They've left some dinner on the table
for us.

10: Yellowknife

PAUL.   It's like this French bistro called *Le Frolic*   [Google directions:
            I think? just down the hill from the hotel   *Ulukhaktok*
            in Yellowknife.   *to Kugluktuk,*
DAN.   That whole flight from Ulu   *Kugluktuk*
            Paul's pitching me a TV show about   *to Yellowknife.]
            life in the Arctic:
PAUL.   *Fawlty Towers* meets
            White Fang!
DAN.   I'm not really writing TV
            shows, Paul.
PAUL.   Then your wife, your wife could write it
            for you!
DAN.   I'm worried about the play, how
            to end it.
PAUL.   I'm not saying it's a good
            French bistro. It's decent. I had dinner
            here on my way up. I'll get a bottle
            of their finest Cabernet. Do you want
            some beer? vodka?
DAN.   How'd you meet your wife, Paul?
PAUL.   My wife?

DAN.   You never mention her. Except
to say she's "changed your life," in your memoir.
Just like you've only told me your mother
is the strongest woman you've ever known.

PAUL.   She's Chinese.

DAN.   Your wife?

PAUL.   No my mother. Yes
my wife's Chinese.

DAN.   She's a photographer,
right? I read that in your book.

PAUL.   I don't talk
about her for a reason.

DAN.   Is she why
you're doing better?

PAUL.   Am I?

DAN.   I don't know
what I thought would happen up here. I'm not
saying I think I failed. Maybe I did,
maybe I failed to get a story, but
I don't know yet. Because in many ways
you're just as fucked up as I'd imagined—

PAUL.   Thank you.

DAN.   In other ways you seem better
than I could ever hope to be.

PAUL.   You sound
kind of disappointed, Dan.

DAN.   What happened
to the ghost of William David Cleveland?
I kept meaning to ask—

PAUL.   What do you mean
what happened to him?

DAN.   Are you still haunted
by him? Does he follow you? Is he here

with us now? Or was that all a story
to sell books.

PAUL.   He's here. He's gotten quieter,
that's true. It could be the meds. I worry
about my son, cosmic retribution
of some kind. I don't think about myself
anymore.

DAN.   When did that change?

PAUL.   I don't know
exactly. I know you were hoping for
an epiphany of some kind. Maybe
an exorcism. I know you wanted
to visit a shaman and have my soul
cleansed—

DAN.   And cleanse myself.

PAUL.   That's not how it works.
You get used to it. It just turns slowly
into something else. It's like when I called
Cleveland's mother—

DAN.   Right that's in your book—

PAUL.   No
that's just book-bullshit. When I wrote that book
I didn't understand it. I didn't
understand the conversation. You should
hear it sometime, remind me to send it
to you when I get home.

DAN.   You recorded
the phone call?

PAUL.   That's right.

DAN.   Why?

PAUL.   Flew to Phoenix,
rented a car. At the Ramada Inn
turned on the AC

PAUL.   and pulled the blinds down   *[Sound:*
and picked up the phone: *answering*

PAUL.   Um yes hello ma'am   *machine*
my name's Paul Watson. This is difficult   *beeping.]*
for me to say. But I took that picture
of your son that day in Mogadishu.
I've wanted to meet you for years, to speak
to you about what happened. And I hope
you might be willing to give me some time
in the next couple of days—

PAUL.   Had some dinner
at the mall, back in the room the phone was—

PAUL.   Hello?

BROTHER.   This is William David Cleveland's
brother.

PAUL.   Oh. —Hi, sir.

BROTHER.   Hi. Can I ask you
never to call my mom again? She called
me crying her eyes out cause you threw her
into a really bad relapse.

PAUL.   Well, sir,
it's just that I've been living with this thing
for more than a decade now—

BROTHER.   You're talking
about that picture you took of my brother
drug through the streets?

PAUL.   That's right. And I'm hoping
if I can understand my place in time
and his place in time, then maybe we could
bury a few things.

BROTHER.   Well, he was no different
than all the people over there right now
in Iraq and Afghanistan. Fighting

for something they believe in, even when
nobody else does.

PAUL.   That doesn't help me
understand him as a person.

BROTHER.   That's him,
that's him as a person.

PAUL.   I know him, sir,
only from that moment. And for my own
mental health—

BROTHER.   He was a kind of weird kid
who didn't match in with nobody. But
he always knew he wanted to protect
people.

PAUL.   Was your father in the navy,
sir?

BROTHER.   He was an engine mechanic.

PAUL.   And
did your brother have a wife?

BROTHER.   Well he had
a couple of them.

PAUL.   And you wouldn't know how
I might go about trying to track down
these women? Or other relatives?

BROTHER.   Nope.

PAUL.   He had some kids I understand.

BROTHER.   Sorry?

PAUL.   He had a few kids.

BROTHER.   —Now are you looking
to do some kind of story again?

PAUL.   Sir,
I just wish we could meet—

BROTHER.   I don't care to
meet you at all.

PAUL.   Do you hate me, sir?

BROTHER.   What?

PAUL.   You hate me, sir, I know it!

BROTHER.   I don't hate
nobody, man!

PAUL.   But—but I dishonored
your brother, that's what haunts me—

BROTHER.   His honor
wasn't tarnished in the least.

PAUL.   Well, sir, see
there's a lot of people who would argue
with you on that point.

BROTHER.   They must not've been
one of the 3,000 people crowding
into a church that could hold only like
a hundred for his funeral. Must not've
been one of the 32 cars following
us all the way to the cemetery,
or the four helicopters with gunships
giving him an escort all the way. They
didn't feel he'd been dishonored.

PAUL.   Others
who know him from my picture—

BROTHER.   I don't care
about your picture! I'm not interested
in discussing it, I'm not interested
in meeting you, and I do apologize
if that offends you, sir—

PAUL.   Could we do this
over email, sir?

BROTHER.   No.

PAUL.   Can't we just meet,
and you can see who I am—!

BROTHER.   Once again
negative.

PAUL.   Sir I have begged, I, I, I
don't understand why—

BROTHER.   You're going to have
to deal with this on your own time.

PAUL.   Your mother
hates me, sir. I read this interview about
that thing in Fallujah where they strung up
the American contractors from that bridge?
And your mother broke down crying and told
the reporter she hated the person
who did it then, like she hates the people
who do it now.

BROTHER.   She was talking about
the people desecrating all of them
bodies.

PAUL.   —No, sir, she was talking about
me, sir! I know it!

BROTHER.   The thing of it was,
when David got shot down and went missing?
since our mom had remarried and taken
a different name, they told his stepmother
he'd been killed in action. We found out while
watching Peter Jennings. When my mother
recognized David's feet. Cause they looked like
his dad's. If it weren't for your picture
we might've never found out.

PAUL.   You must blame
me for that much, sir—

BROTHER.   Man, you don't listen
very well, do you?

PAUL.   Do you want to know
why I did it?

BROTHER.   No.

PAUL.   Why not?

BROTHER.   Explaining
don't change the fact a thing got done.

PAUL.   A week
before, another Black Hawk got shot down,
and kids were parading the body parts
of servicemen through the streets like pennants
at a baseball game. And the Pentagon
denied it. They said it didn't happen.
Because I didn't have a picture.

BROTHER.   Right.

PAUL.   I wasn't a machine, I cared.

BROTHER.   Right.

PAUL.   And
honestly, sir, I believe your brother
would still be alive today if people
had known the truth.

BROTHER.   From my own life I'd say,
and I was in the Air Force for ten years,
I volunteered to go to Somalia
but they wouldn't let me go, cause of work,
where I was. But I can honestly say
I'd have no problem if I'd been the one
in my brother's shoes.

PAUL.   You would've wanted
that picture taken?

BROTHER.   I would've.

PAUL.   Why, sir?
for the reason I just explained or?

BROTHER.   Both,
for the reason you just said and because
you're just doing your job.

PAUL.   Well I'm grateful
to you for saying that.

BROTHER.   Not a problem.

PAUL.   It takes a large weight off. I only wish
the rest of your family felt the same way.

BROTHER.   You're going to have to take my word on that
unfortunately.

PAUL.   Oh yeah no, I won't go
down that route, sir.

BROTHER.   I appreciate that, sir.

PAUL.   I'm just talking about the larger world
here.

BROTHER.   Well the world's fucked up.

PAUL.   Sure.

BROTHER.   Short and sweet,
the world's a fallen place. Ha ha ha.

PAUL.   And
I hope this won't upset you but one thing
that still haunts me is that I heard a voice
when I took that picture. And your brother
warned me: If you do this I will own you
forever.

BROTHER.   Well how do you know David
meant something bad?

PAUL.   He said I will own you
forever—

BROTHER.   Maybe he meant you owe him
something now.

PAUL.   Like what?

BROTHER.   Look, I've got to go
pick up my boy.

PAUL.   Okay sir, I forgot
to ask you your name.

BROTHER.   Ray.

PAUL.   Ray, that's my dad's
name.

RAY.   Ha ha ha.

PAUL.   Sir, please apologize
to your mother for me?

RAY.   Good night.

PAUL.   Good night.

DAN.   The phone's hung up. The hum fades out.

DAN.   Footsteps
on hotel carpeting. The zipping up
of a bag.

DAN.   After dinner we're struggling
through blistering wind,

DAN.   sand snow,

DAN.   to the Hotel
Explorer, this strangely lavish, somewhat
Soviet, high-rise hotel for diplomats
from the south.

PAUL.   I'm going up to Resolute
soon. Where the American scientists hang out
all summer long.

DAN.   —I can't hear you!

PAUL.   I said
I'm doing a story about robot
submarines!

DAN.   That's awesome! Maybe I'll try
for a grant to go with you!

PAUL.   Great!

DAN.   We step
inside the elevator.

PAUL.   I'm leaving
first thing in the morning. Fuck me.

DAN.   My flight's
in the afternoon. So I guess this is
goodbye.

PAUL.   Here's my floor. So.

DAN.   Hey Paul, thank you
for writing back to me for years now. And
for writing back in the first place. It's hard
to explain everything it's meant to me,
to be able to leave my home and go
someplace like this, with somebody like you,
even for a short while.

DAN.   But I don't say
any of that. I say:

DAN.   Paul, I don't know
if this play's going to be any good. But
I'll email it to you when I'm done.

PAUL.   Don't bother,
I won't read it. I can't look back
on all this old stuff anymore, Dan. But
I'm happy you're the one writing it. Bye
now. Safe flight.

DAN.   The elevator closes
and I wonder if I'll ever see him   *[Moving image:*
again.   *snow falling.]*

PAUL.   My deepest apologies, Dan,
for not writing sooner. I'm in Resolute
where I've just destroyed all my computer,
equipment by accident, by dropping
my bag off the side of an icebreaker.   *[Google terrain:*
I simply lost my grip! as we broke through   *Resolute.]*
miles and miles of ice near Taloyoak.

DAN.   I'm working on our play at a theater
in Minneapolis, in a neighborhood

called Little Mogadishu. Somali   *[Google map:*
refugees everywhere. Girls in hijabs   *Minneapolis.]*
walking down the sidewalk. It would be strange
to have you with me here, Paul. I don't know
whether you'd hate it. Or love it.

PAUL.   Dear Dan,
just between me and you, my confessor:
the big news is I'm back in Kandahar.   *[Google Earth:*
It's summer again and the Taliban's   *Kandahar.]*
itching for a fight. The *Toronto Star*
wants its pretty thin coverage here beefed up,
and if I want to keep my wife and son
in new snow boots I need to make myself
valuable to the *Star.* And Canada's
responsible for Kandahar. Truth is
I'm no different than all those Americans
driving their trucks in near suicidal
conditions in Iraq, just to pay off
mortgages in Florida. This is what
I've come to: I'm a mercenary and
a desperate one at that. Just between me
and my confessor. But there's something else:
I feel like Cleveland's happy I've come back,
though I don't know why yet. Maybe you'll come
visit me sometime? Someplace relaxing
like Kabul. Maybe there's a book in it,   *[Google Earth:*
or a play. So what do you say? Will you   *Kabul.]*
come, Dan? I promise I'll keep you as safe
as I can. Though of course nobody knows
what can happen out here. Talk to you soon,
your friend Paul.

End of Play

CPSIA information can be obtained
at www.ICGtesting.com
Printed in the USA
LVOW10s1439090817
544393LV00014B/624/P